MW01071043

The Diving Cats of Bucerias

Robin A. Ladue
Illustrations by Susan H. Morris

2950 Newmarket St., Suite 101-358, Bellingham, WA 98226
206.226.3588 | www.bookhouserules.com

Copyright © 2022 by Robin A. Ladue

All rights reserved. No part of this book may be reproduced, stored in, or introduced into a retrieval system, or transmitted in any form, or by any means (electronic, mechanical, photocopying, recording, or otherwise) without the prior written permission of the publisher.

10 9 8 7 6 5 4 3 2 1

ISBN: 978-1-952483-46-2 (Hardcover)
ISBN: 978-1-952483-47-9 (eBook)

Library of Congress Control Number: 2022909788

Printed in the United States of America

Illustrations by Susan H. Morris

This book is lovingly dedicated to Robert Montoya
and his mother,
Rose Amador LeBeau

and
to Bubby Cat,
my perfect companion

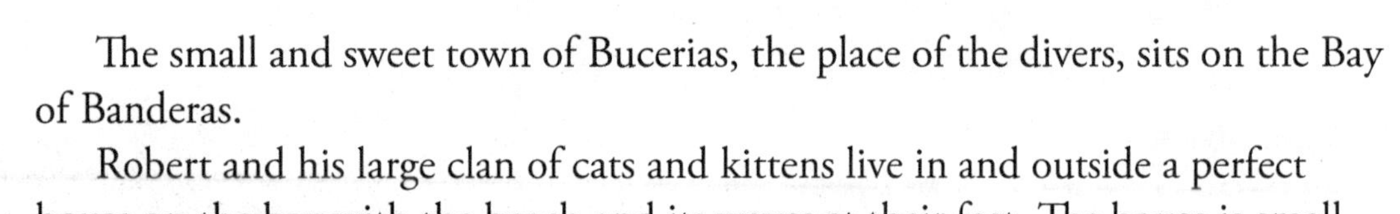

The small and sweet town of Bucerias, the place of the divers, sits on the Bay of Banderas.

Robert and his large clan of cats and kittens live in and outside a perfect house on the bay with the beach and its waves at their feet. The house is small but light and airy and covered in various shades of bougainvillea—pink, red, and orange. It is made of white stucco and painted every year. Wooden window and door frames accent the glistening stucco.

Dozens of tiny cat houses dot the yard, all made to match Robert's house.

As a small child and now as a kind and loving man, Robert has watched the divers of Bucerias bring back their catches. He and his cats love sitting on the beach at night, the lights of the night fisherman casting amazing and dancing shadows on the sand. The cats are entranced by these night riders of the waves and these brave men and women who seek the edible and delicious treasures of the ocean.

At times, schools of flying fish soar by Robert and his minions, making him laugh as the cats run towards the waves, only to run back when washed by the salty sea.

The leader of the cats, the one who rarely leaves Robert's side, is long, muscular, and stunningly handsome and with shiny black fur and a regal manner.

Captain Bubby has long been the lord of the beach. Every morning before Robert awakes, Captain Bubby—followed by his troops of orange and gray tabbies, multi-colored Maine coons, ultra-chic Persians, trim domestic shorthairs, and too many other breeds and colors to name—patrols the beach.

Sitting high on a lifeguard's chair, Captain Bubby sports a white captain's cap with a braided rim perched on his head, he bears white-and-gold striped epaulets on his shoulders, and hard-earned medals cover his chest. Holding a black baton with yellow, red, and white streamers, he calls out directions, meowing so loud the sleeping geckos, iguanas, and birds wake from their sleep and begin to call, making the dawn noisy, as they scream at the cats.

His troops organize themselves into three platoons. Each cat soldier holds whiskers straight out, ears pointed forward, and tails upright and rigid in the warm predawn air. The cats holding the rank of lieutenant inspect their troops and wait for their morning orders.

Once his lieutenants and his troops salute Captain Bubby, the daily duties are ready to begin. Captain Bubby points out the directions for the patrols to go with his tail and with grand flourishes of his baton as the streamers snap in the ocean air.

“Patrol One, go south and get every rat and mouse you find and send them to rodent heaven!

Patrol Two, head to the bridge to town and do the same. Make sure all trash is picked up, too!

Patrol Three, masks and snorkels and air tanks on. I want you out in that warm water, making sure all the garbage and plastics are out and ready for disposal.”

One morning, Robert arose earlier than usual and made his first cup of coffee. He went out onto his porch and looked around for the cats and kittens. Not one was to be found. Never before waking so early, Robert did not know of Captain Bubby's early dawn patrols. He had grabbed a large bag of cat kibbles, intending to put out food for his feline companions, but every cat house was empty.

In a panic, Robert searched the beach, stopping in astonishment as he stared at a platoon of determined and obviously well-trained cats and kittens pulling on diving masks, fins, snorkels, and air tanks. Other cats stood by to assist if needed. When the diving cats were properly suited up, they headed straight into the waves with their tails up and flippers flopping in the sand.

At the sound of a long, loud, and shrill whistle, the diving cats ducked under the water, their tails the last to disappear. Thousands of bubbles marked the spots where the cats did their daily jobs. In a short time, but one that seemed an eternity to Robert, all the cats as one rose to the surface. Each cat pulled an inflatable raft. There were bags of trash and debris in each raft. The cats swam to the beach, rafts bobbing in the waves, and then pulled up on to higher and drier land.

The sky began to brighten, and the birds and geckos sang and clicked so loud that other humans began to stir. From the north and the south, Robert heard small motors. Tiny tractors made their way across the sand, each driven by a large gray cat wearing goggles. Each tiny tractor pulled a trailer, carrying more trash and debris. Straight lines of marching cats followed behind. The procession of tractors came to a stop as the diving cats handed the lines of the rafts to the lower ranks of cats, stripped off their diving gear, stacked it all neatly in piles, and waited with all the other cats for further orders.

Robert stood watching in awe of these patrols and the marvelous bravery of the diving cats. *So this is why the beach of Bucerias is the cleanest in all the land*, he thought.

CAT DVR

Hidden in the lush foliage at the edge of the beach, away from the view of the waking humans, Captain Bubby gave the morning's final commands. The tractors and the loads of trash quickly disappeared into the alleys of Bucerias to be unloaded at the dump. Once this was done, the tiny tractors, trailers, and now cleaned diving gear were stowed in a secret and unmarked garage awaiting the next morning.

With his troops' work done, Captain Bubby waited as his aide-de-camp removed the medals and epaulets and placed them in a black-velvet-lined, polished-cedar case. Captain Bubby then handed his cap and baton to his assistant, Lieutenant TomTom, who carefully placed them into another box. Both boxes were placed in a special compartment on one of the tractors. The aide-de-camp, Lieutenant TomTom, and the tractor driver disappeared down an alley.

Captain Bubby, satisfied with the morning's tasks, strode happily across the beach towards home.

Robert, marveling at the wisdom of Captain Bubby and the strength and commitment of his troops, returned to his house, reaching it before the hungry cats arrived. He filled each bowl with extra food, checked to make sure there were dishes of fresh fish to delight the cats and bowls of water for them. He caught a glimpse of Captain Bubby's tail standing proudly straight, as his army of diving cats, cleaning cats, their drivers and assistants marched up the beach towards home.

Robert quickly ran inside the house, climbed back into bed, and closed his eyes. He heard the soft sound of Captain Bubby's paws on the wood floor. A heavy, warm, and furry body jumped on to Robert's bed, and Captain Bubby curled between Robert's knees. Back to sleep they both fell, dreaming of diving cats, pristine white sands, and clear, clean water where flying fish happily sailed and laughing dolphins rolled in glee.

Someday, when the sky is just starting to turn to the deep blue of another warm day, walk down to the bay and beautiful clean beaches of Bucerias. Look for the small white house, covered in bougainvillea and with full bowls of food and water outside tiny white-washed cat houses. Whisper "Good morning" to the loving and kind man, still sleeping, who cares for the diving cats. Then go and sit on the pretty beach just above where the waves of the Bay of Banderas break.

If you are lucky, you might see Captain Bubby and the diving cats of Bucerias going about their daily chores, ridding the town of rats, cleaning the streets and waters, and making sure the humans have one more day to relax and enjoy a sparkling white sand beach. Thank them and maybe leave a few tasty cat treats. They have earned it!

Acknowledgments

I want to thank Ms. Julie Arrowsmith for her inspiration for this story and her lovely presence on the clean white sands of Bucerias. The place of the divers, the lovely town of Bucerias, has provided peace, joy, and inspiration. I am grateful for every day I have been there on its beaches and in the shade of its palm trees.

Robert showing his approval of *The Diving Cats of Bucerias.*

CPSIA information can be obtained
at www.ICGtesting.com
Printed in the USA
JSHW071018120623
43055JS00002B/3

* 9 7 8 1 9 5 2 4 8 3 4 6 2 *